ZDRAVKA E

LAURA
AND
OTHER STORIES

THIS IS A SNUGGLY BOOK

ISBN: 978-1-64525-153-8

The author would like to thank Quentin S. Crisp for his dedicated editorial work on the current volume.

"Reading his editorial notes was equal to completing a university course in stylistics for me."

LAURA
AND
OTHER STORIES

Zdravka Evtimova is a Bulgarian writer, born in 1959 in Pernik. She is the winner of a number of Bulgarian literary awards, including the H. G. Danov 2021 Award for overall contribution to Bulgarian culture and the Razvitie Literary Award for the best Bulgarian contemporary novel of 2000 for her novel *Your Shadow Was My Home*. Her short story collections and novels have been translated into numerous languages and published in many countries, including France, Italy, Greece, Israel, China and Egypt.

SNUGGLY BOOKS

CONTENTS

LAURA
AND
OTHER STORIES

LAURA

L AURA never haggled over the price of the brandy she bought. She took the bottle, threw the money on the table and that was all. The people in these parts lived on the brandy they sold her, survived like the grass snakes, sticking to the stones and the brown soil that yielded only evil hot peppers and potatoes. Hawthorns, blackthorns and damson trees throve on the wild rocky slopes and if you picked their small fruits you made that yellow brandy that Laura was interested in. The folks raised their children on the money from their demijohns, on wild plums and the sun. The moon didn't give birth to days but to yellow brandy, wild and wicked, smelling of parasol mushrooms, and rattling with the noises ravens made as they spread their wings.

Laura didn't bargain with the guys from the village of Staro. They were skinflints and their shadows reeked of fights and unpaid debts. She drove her ramshackle van to Staro through the knee-deep mud and over the holes in the dirt roads.

She hated all the villagers, but knew she had to put up with one of them, Stoyko. He had two little sons, wild like eels, agile and taciturn, yet he regularly took Laura to one of the empty houses on the periphery of the village. Stoyko had a wife as well, a pale, silent shadow that climbed the hills, picking haws and sloes for the brandy. That woman sucked tomatoes out of the sand and planted cherry trees in between crags and rocks—stunted, undersized saplings that grew there in spite of the savage heat. Laura had seen her many times drag huge tin cans full of duckweedy water to her cherry trees. In summer, there were still some puddles, miserable remnants of the river, which didn't run completely dry.

It was in summer that Stoyko brought Laura to that derelict house; many of the houses remained ownerless if you didn't count the old dogs that outlived their masters. There, amidst the ancient rugs and bleached photographs of moustachioed men, and of women with flocks of children, Laura and Stoyko made love. Laura didn't know what Stoyko did to make the men in shabby trousers sell her their brandy cheap. Perhaps it was his ill temper, which at times scared her, or maybe they did it because he dug the graves for their deceased relatives for a very modest fee. In return for a loaf of white bread, Stoyko dug a most wonderful grave, deep and comfortable, and dead folk joined their maker without a hitch. Some suspected, though, that their maker was not very keen on that village.

They had stones instead of land in their gardens, but then stones were useful, too. Snakes mated under them. The children here became rocks and snakes from an early age. They drank their fathers' brandy, which smelled of ravens, clouds and stolen pine trees. For fuel, men hewed the pines furtively, at night. The plundered hillsides, denuded of trees, shone like bones and produced toadstools. Snakes slept under their flat heads; lizards, thick like ropes, ate the snakes until, unexpectedly, the sky exploded and started unloading rain on the potato fields.

Rain after rain, and no break for two months until the river was born again. It rushed, rumbling, sweeping roots and bushes from the earth, wrenching sand from beneath the sitting rooms of the houses. The water dragged along drowned snakes and lizards, and Laura remembered it had mixed with the brandy in the demijohns. After the rain, the river smelled of pines and ravens, the brandy was the colour of dead snakes, but she and Stoyko were very happy in that ownerless house in spite of the downpour. Everything around them was wet and Laura wondered if the puddles on the floor were water or brandy. She had seen Stoyko's wife in the mud, erect like a lamppost under the rain, watching.

Laura had chosen Stoyko for two reasons: because of his thick brandy, and because most of the other villagers were old men who did not look at her the way Stoyko did. At times, she thought of his sons. Last year they went to school by bus, then they had to walk, for petrol was too expensive. Children here were a true rarity, like the fish in the river that was always running dry. Unlike the fish, however, the water snakes learned to live on dry land and mated with the real snakes. Thousands of hybrids from these couplings were born and swam in the rain. When Laura drove the brandy to Pernik, she smelled of pines, of mushrooms and snakes.

In the beginning, she had sold it in the main square, squatting down behind a makeshift stall in the form of an ancient table. She had pilfered it from an old house whose landlord was a feeble mutt. Laura always managed to push up the price, then checks started and inspectors wanted to see her permit, which she didn't have. So she rented a cellar from Nenko, a mechanic who could make a car out of an old vacuum cleaner if he was not too drunk. Laura paid him the rent in brandy, but not the brew that smelled of swelling rivers. She gave him a glass of the hogwash brew she bought from the gypsies in the village of Vladimir. Those gypsies made brandy out of cabbage leaves and turnips, or maybe they used cinders to produce their concoction. Those that drank it often had headaches, and their poor mugs turned blue. Nenko's mug, however, never turned blue; he felt no pain and was quite comfortable with the Vladimir brew she gave him. He told her once, "I'd die for you." But he could not love when drunk. The one thing he was capable of was fixing up broken old boneshakers.

Laura sold her brandy in thick, opaque glasses, also pinched from the house of the old mutt. A disordered line of men, bluish in the face, formed down the flight of stairs to her cellar. The men downed the Vladimir brandy contentedly, since she sold it dirt cheap. When Laura remained in the mechanic's cellar for a week, Stoyko arrived in Pernik to visit her. She could only guess how much he had squandered to reach Pernik. He rushed to her cellar and thundered, "Where's the other guy?"

He was spoiling for a fight with the men in the line. As far as he was concerned, Laura had probably cheated on him. She locked and bolted the door then she made love to him while the guys waited humbly for her to open the cellar again. They desperately wanted their thirty-five cent glasses of Vladimir. Stoyko could hardly bear them all the same.

"Let's run away to Spain," he urged Laura. "We'll plant damson trees there, we'll distil brandy and we'll make the Spaniards blue in the face like us. Or why not come back home and stay with me?"

In Pernik, there were no buyers for the thick brandy with the sun and clouds in it, but Laura enjoyed its yellow presence behind her back. There were the river, the mushrooms and Stoyko's two sons in its amber depths. Laura had seen the boys write swear words on her van. Once, they punctured all four of its tyres with nails and the van lay down on the road like a dead cow. Then Laura watched the father thrash the kids with a stick he snapped off from the stunted cherry tree his wife had planted. It looked as if he had beat them with the tin cans the scrawny woman dragged along in the scorching heat of July. Their eyes fixed on their mother's face, the boys had not tried to evade the blows. When Stoyko was gone they threw stones and cow dung at Laura. Strange, Laura was out of sorts on account of that woman, though she didn't do anything but stick out from the ground like a goal in an empty football field. An open goal that nobody cared for, that was what that woman was. Laura felt sorry for her, but not enough to give her a bill from the bundle she had in her pocket after she sold the Vladimir brandy.

She felt sorry because her own mother lived alone in one of the houses beneath the Black Peak. Her father had moved in with a young woman Laura liked and played backgammon with from time to time. Laura's mother was sparing of words, her face closed like a wall. Perhaps her father was right to move in with Darina. Darina who smoked like a brick field, sang pop hits, jumbling up tunes and rhymes in a hot unbearable mess. She sold vegetables in the market square in Pernik and her mouth never ceased babbling even if she had a cigarette in it. Laura's father listened to her, smiling, happy that he could hear a human being speak. Whenever his second wife shut up to light another cigarette, her father's face looked worried.

When Laura was little, her mother had chased the boys away from their backyard. The girls were afraid of her, too, because of the wall she had instead of a face. If Laura had wanted to kiss a boy she had had no choice but to walk to the neighbouring village. Rumours had it Laura's mother dabbled in black magic. Actually, all she had done was to buy a cheap plastic icon to which she prayed day and night, petitioning for her daughter to become rich. Laura's mother was taciturn, but her power of speech broke down completely when she found her husband with a woman, their neighbour of many years. The man had simply called in for a chat, but the woman's words had sunk into his heart and he had kissed her. Laura's mother lapsed into silence thereafter and neighbours said it was not an accident that toadstools sprouted up in her backyard, slugs infested her garden, and under the ground the moles were so numerous they ate even the rocks. It was only the brandy in her house that was really good.

One day, Yani came to buy brandy from Laura's cellar. In fact, he was a nameless regular who had been buying the normal brandy for some time. It was only this time, however, a long time after his first visit, that she learnt his name was Yani. On this day he paid for a gallon of the sickening Vladimir brew and started drinking it mulishly, his back propped against the wall, tears welling up in his eyes. His face became blue, even his black eyes turned blue, and Laura feared he might breathe his last right there in her cellar.

"Why are you doing this?" Laura asked him, noticing that in spite of his livid complexion the young man was as handsome as an angel. He had dark hair and a face that looked like a prayer to her, the face she had been dreaming of while her van got stuck in the mud of the dirt roads. She had seen that face while Stoyko moaned he'd do anything she wanted, forgetting it was raining and that drowned grass snakes floated down the river. Yani's dark, drunken tears dripped into the cheap Vladimir brew as Laura kissed him.

"She's gone," the lad muttered, as if belatedly answering her question.

Laura asked him what his name was and he didn't know. She had been dreaming all her life that someone would forget his name because of her, but that had never happened. Her own name was notorious in the whole district and when villagers saw her van, she knew they said, "The leech will be here again." Women substituted various insulting words for her name and Stoyko's wife was said to be seized with a fit beside the pot of soup she cooked if one of her sons mentioned Laura's name by mistake.

Laura took out the lad's wallet and his identity card told her his name was Yani. She kissed him again and slammed the door in the faces of the men who waited in a quiet line for her brandy. They spoke softly so that one might suppose they were in a church or waited outside a surgeon's office. (Sometimes Laura awarded a "Vladimir" to the most tractable one among them. A Vladimir meant a free beer bottle of the gypsy brew. The lucky man who got it would sweep the floor and smile at Laura. She would watch him closely, fearing he might pinch one of her precious opaque glasses.) Although the door was locked, Yani did not stop drinking and sobbing while Laura kissed him. He looked so beautiful, Laura made up her mind to give him a bottle of her true amber brandy. It was all August mornings, damsons and warm winds. The damson trees sucked life out of the crags and infused rocks into her brew. There was gold in the hills, and surely it squeezed its way into her demijohns.

Laura admired Yani's chest so much she gave him the best of her amber treasure. She had never been so impressed before, not even when her mother had given her a pair of green corduroys. When she first wore them, the villagers had wondered if it was really Laura, or some pretty girl from Pernik who had lost her way and chased the wind amidst the snakes and lizards in their backyards. Laura's mother had remained in her room, silent like the dead grass on the hills.

One day Laura had discovered that her mother had a mania for building a wall around her house. Her neighbours kept away from her even when she went to buy bread, so the woman started piling up rocks round her backyard. She dragged together stones, thorns, and stray brambles, all of which were welcomed by the lizards as nesting places. When Laura came to see her mother, she lit up, if it was possible for a wall to light up. Her mother hugged her and Laura wondered how this woman survived here in the sun. The cherries had withered, the peppers had become dry like flint and the moles had turned the garden into a wasteland of craters and molehills. Her mother had a nanny goat named Hope, a bitch named Hope, too, an old TV set and a calendar. Every time Laura visited her after that, the heap of stones around the house was larger. Laura worried over her mother's sanity.

"How's your mother?" her father asked, taking a guilty look at her shabby, scorched backyard. "They say she's off her head."

"She's okay," Laura said.

Once she found her mother talking to a young man whose face was very different from Yani's. This man's face was no icon and cried for no girl that was gone. This man was blond, colourless, and thin like the withered tomato stalks behind the house. He constantly dug the garden and planted beans, looking more and more like the moles to which he talked in a soft, imploring voice. He spoke to Hope, the bitch, and to Hope, the nanny goat, and her mother listened, smiling. Her mother appeared happy she could hear a living thing speak. Then her mother asked the scraggly man to tell her fairy tales in the evening. Laura was rendered speechless. She didn't think much of his tales, yet she started to suspect she fancied the man. She gave him some of her amber brandy, a teacup, and asked him to come and catch grass snakes under the stones with her. (People gossiped, said that her mother caught grass snakes and baked them to cure her silence and aching knees with their skins.) The blond man took a gulp of the yellow thunder of Laura's brandy and his transparent face became purple right away. "What did you do to him!" her mother cried out, terrified.

That purple face told Laura the blond one was not a real man and had most probably visited her mother to have his body healed with grass snake's skin. Laura left the two of them alone. She stopped asking herself why that scrawny little guy had crawled out from the pile of stones and thorns surrounding her mother's backyard. Laura's mother treated him for a month before his face healed and became again white and soft like a girl's. One evening, Laura found the two of them sitting in front of a bucket of milk. Hope, the bitch, sniffed at a heap of raw snake's meat. Hope, the nanny goat, bleated softly. It was pouring with rain, and animals and people were sharing the sitting room.

It was autumn, the best time to buy brandy in these parts. So many toadstools had sprouted around the thorns and stones in her mother's backyard that Laura was scared. When she examined them carefully, she gasped. They were all edible mushrooms. The scrawny man and her mother drank milk and smiled at each other. It was so frightful and so amazing that Laura could not believe it. Some guys in the village said the man was a brandy merchant, but that was certainly not true: the only brandy merchant in the village was Laura.

"What's your name?" Laura asked the scrawny guy, but he did not answer. He had forgotten what his name was and sat there, smiling at her mother. Rain poured from the torn sky, but the blond one did not see it. He looked at her mother, not even telling her fairy tales. He looked at her and didn't know his name.

Yani, too, had forgotten his name because of a girl. After Laura locked the door of the cellar, she took him behind the only demijohn of yellow thunder. There she admired his magnificent face and loved him. He couldn't concentrate, though. He told her time and again about the girl. She was so beautiful that it stopped raining whenever she showed up. This made no difference to Laura. She loved him on the mat Stoyko had given her. Perhaps his wife had woven it years ago. Stoyko never forgot his name. He had grown wild and intractable and refused to drink the amber brandy. He was afraid he might fall asleep while he was with Laura.

One day, after Laura had taken Yani to her amber-filled demijohn in the cellar, the rain stopped and someone knocked at the door. This had never happened before. No one was allowed to bang on Laura's door, not even Nenko, the mechanic she paid two Vladimir bottles a month. Nenko drank his Vladimir, cleaned the cobwebs in the cellar and swept the floor. Whoever this is, he'll pay through the nose, Laura thought and opened up.

A woman stood before her, a woman so pretty that the men who waited in an irregular line had suddenly sobered. Laura had not seen such a beautiful woman before, although women from the hills of the grass snakes and damson trees were usually pretty. Even Stoyko's wife, jutting out like a sword, watching them from the backyard of the house, was pretty.

"Go away!" Laura said to the woman. At that point she saw Yani's face light up. Yani's face, as beautiful as an icon that Laura had just kissed, glowed and smiled. The woman smiled as well. She smiled so thinly that the brandy in the demijohns throbbed. Laura's mother and the blond, colourless man had smiled at each other like that by the bucket with the milk. Yani rushed to the girl.

"Yani!" Laura shouted. "Yani!" But he had forgotten his name again.

When Laura drove back with the van to buy up the brandy in the village of Staro, she saw a thing that amazed her. Stoyko stood alone in the middle of his backyard, under a big bleached umbrella. "She went away with the children," Stoyko said to her.

His house looked exactly as it had two years ago, a low, one-storey building, its backyard swimming in the rain; no garden, just puddles and mud. The green tomatoes had rotted on their stalks, decaying peppers, grey like the clouds, hung to the sodden ground. It was not necessary to plod their way to the house on the outskirts of the village. Laura moved in with Stoyko. His sons' school timetable was still glued to the wall; their old shoes and his wife's apron lay on the floor in the kitchen. On the first day, Stoyko collected the odds and ends and threw them out of the house. A new garbage heap had sprung up behind the rocks and branches Laura's mother had piled around her backyard. There, amidst the mushrooms that grew like mad, Stoyko dumped all the old junk. Stoyko and Laura didn't go out of the house for a whole week. One of the neighbours brought them food and drink from the village grocery store, ample supplies of bread, sausages and cheese. Love didn't happen when one was hungry.

The neighbour took care of them diligently because Laura had given him a pail of the thunder brandy. The man would have hauled the whole town of Pernik to them for a much smaller demijohn. Stoyko, wild with the brandy and with Laura, smiled in his sleep. But he did not forget his name on account of her.

Then Laura bought up all the brandy from the villagers. She took the whole summer, the hills they had been tramping, their damsons, kernels and sloes. She bought the hours during which the men had strained their ears listening to the gurgling noises in the casks, waiting for the amber and thunder to trickle into the brandy still. She loaded up the van with the demijohns and was off to Nenko, the mechanic, who had already scoured and scrubbed the cellar for her. Its clean floor shone like a mirror. Her regular clients had already fallen down the flight of stairs and waited for her, money in fists, ready for their Vladimirs.

When Laura drove back to the village of Staro, she saw a rusty chain and a padlock hanging on the front door of Stoyko's house. One of the windows had been boarded up. Behind it was the room where he had eaten a mountain of bread and sausages, and had made love happen as often as the raindrops in the rainstorm.

"Stoyko!" Laura shouted out. "Stoyko!"

Nobody answered her. The dog that had been hanging about the house while the neighbour took care of their food had vanished. A crumpled piece of paper was nailed to the wall. Some words were printed in pencil on the scrap. There were no commas, no full stops, just enormous spaces, like toadstools, between the warped letters:

> - k i d s a r e h u n g r y i a m w i t h t h e m s t o y k o

The money Laura had made, the yellow rain, the rust of the chain on the door, weighed her down. She stood rigid, her lips stiff, her eyes cold and remote like the autumn wind.

THE TALE I'LL TELL YOU

YOU shouldn't have done it, Janna.

Happiness is a simple thing, you said. Happiness is a patch of shade where you look at me. But there is no shade in Trun. In summer there is no grass like the grass you see in your picture books. The dust is knee-deep and it is so hot your heels bleed, and there are flies in the thick air that drink water from your eyes. The sun is so red you can't look at it. The trees are all withered.

Anyway, I won't be in Trun to see you anymore, Janna. Yesterday Kin came to my father. They talked for a while. You know what happens when Kin comes to someone's shack.

When Kin left, my mother cried and Father didn't look me in the eye.

"Xav,'" he said, "they'll come to take you tomorrow. You can say your goodbyes to your brothers." Then he lit a cigarette. His eyes lingered in the dust as he spoke: "Kin said he'd bring you back to us. He told me they won't cut your face."

Mother was silent. She wiped her eyes with the back of her hand, then she went behind the shack. We'd never seen her cry. She came back carrying our old goat. She'd killed it and there was blood on her hands. If Father had only scolded her, it might still have been better. What would the other kids eat now? that's what he should have said. But he said nothing. My brothers were all looking at me, saying nothing. My sisters were there, looking away, all saying nothing.

"I'll cook a stew for you, son," Mother said, pressing the dead goat to her puny chest.

A week ago, after the sandstorm, one of the shepherds found a dead man. The man's throat was slashed. He was from the Oshav clan and his body was strong. I knew this man—he used to collect dry thorns for his goats on the mountain. Happiness is a simple thing, you said: daylight and you looking at me.

If one of the Oshav men got killed, one of our Bogoin men had to be killed. Blood for blood, it was as simple as that.

"Samur, you'd better decide which of yours will be the one," Kin had said to Father. "I'll come to collect him after midday bread. He has to be the same age as the dead Oshav guy. They don't want an old man and they don't want a sick man. You know what will happen if you don't give one of yours."

Mother knew what would happen. The Oshavs would come and kill my seven brothers one by one. They wouldn't kill my sisters. There were other things you could do to a woman, things worse than death.

There were too many mouths that wanted to eat on that mountain. And there was dust, knee-deep, hot, brown powder, in which thorns grew. But the thorns were too scant to go around. There were goats that ate them and not enough water to nourish new roots. Neither court nor law extended to Trun. No one had ever seen a living judge. Kin would come to take whoever was chosen after midday bread. Two days later, Kin would drive a cart carrying the body back to the family. The dead man's brothers and sisters would wash him, and in the evening, when the heat was not so fierce, they would drink tea. The Oshavs, like us, made tea from the thorns. It was bitter. It made you dizzy and you saw things that were not there, but you slept. You slept like a stone, and you didn't see the body of your dead brother.

"Xav," Father said to me, "you are the weakest. Whatever you do, you won't live long. But don't show the Oshavs you are sick, my son. Go and pick the thorns. Let the Oshavs see you picking them."

You know there's something wrong in my chest, Janna. You've seen me cough and wheeze. If I go out when it rains, I choke on the wind. I fall to my knees and I pray for the rain to turn to drizzle. Otherwise I can't go out for a walk. Father was right. One way or the other I wouldn't last long. But, Janna, you know happiness is a simple thing. Some wind, some thorns for our tea, and you. And if I weren't sick, they wouldn't let me come to your shack, would they?

"Xav is a sick wreck," your mother said. "And he's got a golden mouth. He thinks up good tales. There's no harm in listening to him."

Then I learned happiness was a simple thing. "What do you have in that bag, Xav, more of your sweet lies?" your mother would say.

I had none, but the dust was full of summer tales, and there were thorns simmering for tea. And in winter, there was snow piled higher than the shacks, and there were thorns again, burning in the hearth. Maybe I was to blame for everything. I taught you to believe in the nonsense I spoke to you and your sisters.

You shouldn't have done that, Janna.

Midday passed, and the stew Mum made with the goat she'd killed waited on the table. I asked myself what the other kids would eat later. There would be no milk for the new baby now and no meat if someone fell sick. My brothers looked at me. They didn't eat. Father and Mother didn't eat either.

My sisters looked at me, too, the youngest one sobbing softly, the others quiet. I thought about the fairy tales. Snow was bread, Mother had told me, and dust was flour. The best flour you could find on Trun Mountain.

"No crying," Father said. "Eat."

But we knew Kin was coming.

"Run away," Mother had said to me the night before. "We can bring you something to eat."

"He's sick." Dad's voice crawled like dust over dust. "They'll kill him and they'll kill us too. Better eat the stew she cooked for you, son."

We waited and waited and Kin didn't come.

"What does he want?" Dad grumbled. "Perhaps he expects us to take you to him?" It couldn't be! That had never happened before. No man in his right mind would do such a cowardly thing.

I tried not to think about it, Janna. I remembered when it had rained. Not when the rain was falling and the valley was a cauldron of steaming red mud and black clouds, but after the rain when the flowers sprouted. Red and blue and yellow, they grew on the roofs of the shacks and they shot up under our feet, so many that we couldn't see the sand.

"Xav," you said, "these flowers are just like the tales you told us. Look at them. Happiness is a simple thing."

If I hadn't been sick your father wouldn't have let me talk to you. Your mother wouldn't have brought tea for me. And I told you a lie once, Janna.

"Take a handful of the wet mud after the rain is over and knead it well. Put some petals from the flowers in that mud and let it dry. Then give that ball of dry clay to the person you want to be happy . . . and he will be." It was a lie, Janna. I found a ball of dry clay in front of our shack. My sisters told me that you made it for me.

"I'll go instead of you, Xav," Father said.

We all knew it was impossible. The dead Oshav guy was young and strong. Father was old. I was the weakest in the whole village and the cold in the winter would carry me off soon; if not, the heat in summer would.

"But nobody can tell such beautiful tales, Xav," you said. "You understand what the dust says and you know what the wolves think. And you know where the flowers go after the rain stops."

"Chew this when they start beating you," Father said. "Chew and it won't hurt."

"Xav, run away, son! I won't give you to them!"

"But the village has made its decision, woman," Father said.

"We'll run away from the village."

"Then our own clan will catch us. Your own brothers will stone you to death, woman."

"I don't care. I won't give them Xav."

"If they don't kill me, Mother, I won't make it through the winter."

"You'll make it, son, you'll make it. You can take my word for it. Run, Xav!"

Then Father went up to her, he walked very slowly to her, as he always did. He went slowly up to her and hit her.

"Say one more word and I kill you," he told her.

"Kill me," she said. "Kill me. I won't give them Xav."

Father's hand went limp.

No one ate from the goat stew and the shack was full of the most beautiful aromas. My sisters were quiet. The midday eating should have been finished some time ago. I knew it by the shadows of the peaks, which crept on the ground and mingled with the dust.

Kin came in. No one had heard him drag his feet on the gravel. He usually dragged his feet and kicked the dust when he came to collect one of us for the Oshavs. He had been the death of more people than there were now living in the village.

"Xav can stay with you," he said slowly. "Now give me a bowl of your stew for the good news I've brought you."

Mother gave a sob. My brothers stood up.

"Don't make fun of me," Father wheezed. "You are an important man, but it's my house."

"Keep your sickly son at home," Kin said. "Somebody else went to the Oshavs instead of him."

The silence was thicker than the heat. Father's face was grey. Mother's cracked lips bled.

"Give me that stew," Kin said.

"Who went instead of him?" Father croaked.

"You wouldn't want to know."

"Tell me who went instead of him, and I'll give you some stew."

Kin's face sweated. His lips were wet with saliva. He swallowed a couple of times.

"Janna went instead of him," Kin said. "Ran away from her family. Her father, old Sazmi, cropped her hair. Shame on them! That girl must have been mad. The whole family is disgraced."

I could not hear Kin's words. I saw you picking the flowers after that big rain, and I saw you make a big heart of clay with the flower petals in it. "You'll be healthy some day, Xav," you said. Janna, why did you do that? I can no longer see the dust, and I cannot see the mountain. I see what they are doing to you. I wish you were dead. I wish I was dead.

"Janna is young and strong," Kin said.

"She won't die quickly," Father said.

"She's young and she'll last a long time," Kin said. "Each one of the Oshav lads will have a piece of her as long as she lasts."

I hit Kin as hard as I could. I hit him, and I hit him and I hit him as long as I could see him. Then there was dust in my mouth and blood in my eyes. Janna, I see you in the evening when the sky sleeps. I see you in the daylight. Happiness is a simple thing. In the heat it suddenly rained. Clouds and skies and dust mingled and the valley was a lake of red mud and stones. Goats were drowned in the whirlpools. And then the sun shone. There were flowers—red and blue and yellow and lilac, all the mountain was flowers.

I'll come and find you, Janna. I'll come to the Oshavs and I'll find you. And I will tell you the most beautiful tale.

GOOD FIGURE,
BEAUTIFUL VOICE

I rarely talked to anybody. I had always lived in unstable silence, the winters that hurled snow and rain at my windows passing unnoticed and unnecessary. Probably, my new next-door neighbour thought I was an odd bird. I could tell that by the way she stared at me when we met at the grocery store. I'd been living in this neighbourhood for five months. I chose the room, tucked away down a narrow street, for its north-facing window. All the houses here were small and you could scarcely see them in the fog. There was fog everywhere: on the roofs, in the trees, in my hair and coat. The sun gave birth to fog instead of mornings.

I thought I was bad company so I kept myself to myself, going for interminable strolls in the wasteland beyond the only bridge in town. I tried to remember the outlines of the low, squat buildings as they slowly dissolved into the afternoons like memories of a snowstorm. Sometimes young men would whistle at me. The town was not big. People knew each other and I was a complete stranger—a new poster advertising a concert on the main street.

I guessed the townsfolk unanimously mistrusted me when they learned what I did for a living. Even before the end of the first month of my tenancy in the narrow street, I gained an established notoriety as an unbearable teacher of mathematics. I wanted the students to prove theorems and solve problems. Otherwise, I didn't speak much to them. And on the very first day at school, I caught two lads cribbing from finely folded sheets of paper they had tucked up their sleeves. Unfortunately for myself and others, I saw and heard most of what happened in the classroom. I could almost always tell when a student was trying to cheat. When I was a little girl, even Grandma could not trick me into believing that Dad had gone on a long business trip to Sweden to make money for us. I knew he had divorced Mother. A year after that, when Mother promised she would come back home to see me after Uncle Gerard took her to hospital for some blood tests, I knew she wouldn't. I tried keeping a stiff upper lip, but all I managed was to bite my lower one, which had long ago become exceedingly thin and colourless.

The only place in the town where I talked was the classroom where I tested my students. I hated to see students copying from their neighbours. I took the neatly folded sheets of paper with the scribbled formulae from their fists and kept them on my desk. I supposed it was mortifying to be stared at by your maths teacher. My classes hated me—I saw it in their eyes—and so everything I said sounded short, stiff and formal, even to my own ears. Every time I encountered a student I knew, as he sauntered by, I felt awkward, the fog making me freeze in my tracks even when I was at my favourite place, in front of the bridge, the wilderness whispering to me.

One Wednesday, I asked one of the students to prove the theorem about raising the diagonals of a rhombus to the second power. I watched him closely as he tore the sheet from his textbook and started for the blackboard. He began to copy the theorem from the sheet, not even trying to conceal what he was doing. He printed the words slowly, unfalteringly, peeking at me now and then over his shoulder. Even before he had finished, I gave him a poor mark.

"Sit down," I said.

He remained in front of the blackboard, calm, tall, writing the formulae, pausing to rub the chalk powder from his fingers. He copied the theorem to the end and bowed to the class. The students applauded vigorously, some laughing, others smirking. I didn't know what to do with my eyes and my hands; if I panicked I'd start to cry. It turned out I had dropped my own piece of chalk some time ago and I saw it at my feet on the floor. It was very hot in the room. Words failed me. I stood there, mute, humiliated. I was scared my voice would sound gravelly and they would all dissolve into laughter. They simply continued to watch, perfectly silent. I staggered to the blackboard and gripped another piece of chalk, then started dictating slowly, the words dead on my lips, "The diagonals of a rhombus . . ."

The students listened. I hoped they had not noticed how dry my voice was, or perhaps they were accustomed to it that way. Suddenly the boy I had given a poor mark jumped from his desk and sent his bag crashing to the floor.

"Excuse me," he said, strutted to my desk, took my piece of chalk and left without closing the door.

All the rest were silent, watching me. I checked the boy's name in the register. He was called Rogier.

That day I had four more lessons, each weighing a ton. I felt pulverised; in fact, every day I left school exhausted as if I had dragged heaps of rock from the slate quarry in the hills to the mountain top. As I exited the school building, I had a headache. The schoolyard, the shops and the birches were brown silhouettes, and the town was whispers and the whirring of motors through which my headache and I navigated. At last I reached my narrow street where the houses were neat and immobile mussel shells.

The small square in front of the cottage where I lived was my medicine. It ended abruptly at the foot of a hill overgrown with shrubs and thorns that merged with the autumn evening and its starless sky. I wanted a cup of tea, and I wanted my warm room where I could forget the classroom, the town and the theorems. Every evening I lit all the lamps and celebrated the absence of fog and blackboards around me. I had counted the steps that separated my room from the schoolyard. It was pleasant counting the yards to go before my cup of strong tea.

Suddenly, somebody whistled at me. I jumped. I rarely met people in my narrow street; silence here felt like the ocean floor. The face, which bobbed up in the mist before me, jangled my nerves. It was Rogier—the student I had given a poor mark.

I walked past him, aware of strange noises. I soon realised there were two more young men with Rogier who I didn't know. I quickened my pace, forbidding myself to look back, feeling their words and breath on my neck. I could hear their light footfalls behind my back. When I was a little girl my grandmother used to leave me at home by myself while she gave lessons in maths to students at their homes. I was accustomed to silence and I knew it was my friend. The three of them tailed me. They had become silent like the pavement under their feet. I had lived alone and I was not afraid of footsteps in the dark. I reached the front door of the house where I lived, turned around and looked at them. They stared back.

I entered the house and closed the door. Inside, it was quiet and warm.

On the following day, Rogier walked out of the classroom in the middle of my lesson. He had been humming a familiar-sounding tune for quite a time. When I asked him to stop he winked at the class, then left.

In the afternoon, Rogier and the other two trailed after me while I walked along the grey-paved street. I wished I could dash off, but I repeated to myself that I was not scared. It was dark and I could hear their shoes against the pavement. One of the three lads, the tallest among them, with a swarthy face, overtook me, halted and looked me in the eye.

"I'd like to tell you something," he said. "My name is Boris." His face, long and thin, almost touched mine. He cleared his throat.

"I have never met a girl like you. You have a good figure." His dark eyes measured me slowly. "You have a beautiful voice. Your eyes are beautiful."

Derision oozed thickly from his words. Rogier and the other lad were only a step away from us, watching me, sniggering. Boris was sniggering, too. Suddenly, he let out a loud guffaw. I did not mind that. I could endure anything. I looked at him then turned and continued down the street. The houses huddled in the dusk, making it jagged and menacing. I reached the small square, the shrubs and wilderness. This time my well-lit room and my cup of strong tea were no good.

In the morning I had a headache; during the five lessons with my classes it became excruciating. I dictated the problems and repeated the theorems, trying to ignore the waves of uneasiness as best I could. Finally the lessons were over and I walked slowly out of the schoolyard.

The three lads were waiting for me at the beginning of my narrow street. They roared with laughter the minute they saw me. I hurried past them, trying to remain composed.

"I'd like to tell you something," one of them shouted. I didn't stop. I noticed his eyes were the colour of the fog—watery, cold. "I have never met a girl like you before. You have a good figure. You have a beautiful voice. . ." Suddenly he was short of breath and looked at Rogier and Boris for support. I didn't wait for the remaining part of the explanation.

"Will Rogier be the next one?" I asked.

My question was greeted with jeers. I ignored them. My eyes were beautiful, I knew that. I left the boys where they were and walked down the narrow street feeling their eyes on my back.

I went home and tried to sleep. The town was blue behind my windowpanes. In the morning, before I went to work, I found the three lads in the square with the bridge. Boris and Rogier came striding along to meet me.

"I'd like to tell you something," Rogier said. He looked away, blushing.

"I won't listen to you," I told him.

"I have never met a girl like you," he started. "You have a good figure. Your voice is beautiful. Your eyes are beautiful, too . . ." Then he didn't know what to say. He looked at the bridge for help, hoping I'd go away. I waited.

"Her hair is beautiful, too," Boris prompted him. His words were so sharp and edgy they seemed to sting.

"Tomorrow I'll wait for you at 7 p.m. in front of my house," I said.

Rogier coughed. The swarthy Boris stared, surprised.

"She's up to something," he muttered.

Perhaps my neighbour had seen me and was wondering what I was discussing with these young men. I took a step forward. I had to go to work.

"What did you say?" Rogier asked.

I did not answer.

"Hey, what did you say?" Boris cried out, his voice indignant. "You'll wait for me, is that it?"

I didn't answer him. I knew I had one thousand steps to go before I reached the classroom.

"What did you say?" Boris caught up with me.

"Tomorrow at 7 p.m.," I said, so quietly he had to bend if he wanted to hear my words.

That day I examined many students. I spoke slowly, avoiding their eyes. I didn't look at Rogier.

At 7 p.m. sharp I was in front of my house. Boris had already arrived. The other two boys were a couple of yards away from him, hiding behind a clump of pine trees. This time they were not laughing. They watched me. I watched them, too, and I was not scared.

Boris waited, his hands thrust into his pockets. I came up to him, nodded, studying his face. It was very smooth and dark. He kept silent as I watched him run his fingers through his hair. It was black and thick.

"Hi," he said at last.

The other two boys had pushed aside the branches of the pine trees. They waited, ready to start sniggering. Suddenly I hated them.

"Stop fidgeting," I told Boris.

He stared, confused. I caught him by the shoulders, stood on tiptoe and kissed him.

I hated Rogier and the other lout. I hated the young man I had just kissed, and I couldn't stand the fog. I had already taken my revenge. No sound of steps came after me, no one guffawed. The fog and the pavement were peaceful. The houses smiled.

In the morning on the following day, I entered the classroom. It was peaceful there, too. The students looked at me peculiarly, their eyes quiet like my evening cup of tea. As always, I started the lesson with a new theorem, leaving a storm of chalk dust in my wake. Rogier smiled and that made me feel awkward. I felt ashamed of myself and stopped myself from turning back to look at the students.

After the lessons were over, Boris waited for me near the bridge. His two friends were not with him.

PARABLE OF STONES

"LISTEN up, girl. Men are stones, the lot of them, and there's no exception to this rule," she says. "It's up to you if you have him as a huge millstone tied around your neck, so you plunge into the river and drown, or you throw him in the mud and step on him, so your shoes don't get dirt on them."

She is a middle-aged woman and her name is known throughout Struma Valley, Bulgaria. If business is bad or your love life has stalled, if you're sick at heart or tired of the world's dead weight, you look for her and ask her advice. The charge: ten levs.

"I've made up my mind to leave my husband," I tell her. "I need to be away from him, but he's not a bad man."

"Of course he's not a bad man! He's a rotten man. Pack up and leave him! Guys are two a penny, take it from me, and each one of them is after your scalp. He skins you, and he goes and boasts to his cronies you've cried your heart out for him. He's not a bad man, eh! Then why are you talking to me? What did you shell out ten levs for?"

"I don't know."

"Listen to me now. I'll tell you a story, and I hope you'll understand once and for all there're no good-natured guys out there. They are rubble and roof-tiles. If you're clever you'll chuck your husband in the dirt, or even better, you'll hurl him at another man's head. Listen now and don't interrupt me, girl."

She begins to speak softly as if I am not there.

"I was flaming like a torch, going out of my mind with love for a young feller, a petty trader who sold brandy in the town of Pernik. One day he came to my backyard and looked at my orchard, but I doubt he saw anything in particular. He wasn't paying attention to the trees, you can take my word for it; he gave me the eye instead.

"'You're very pretty,' he said.

"'Go and spin yarns somewhere else.' I wasn't going to play his game. 'We've got plenty of mirrors in our house.'

"'But you are! Why don't you believe me?'

"'What do you want?' I asked, mincing no words. I knew what he was after. I possessed a whole slope, every square yard of it planted with plum trees. You see, I was a wily thing, and I still am; it's true I have freckles on my cheeks, but this doesn't mean I don't have a hard nose for business.

"I'd bought a long hill, then another one, so I held all the plum trees in the district in my hands. The truth is in the plums, you should never forget that, my dear girl. Plums are brandy in the future tense.

"'You are very intelligent,' the petty trader said.

"'I am,' I agreed. 'If you're here to buy my plums, let's speak business. I don't have time for anything else.'

"'I want five hundred kilos of plums.'

"'How much are you ready to pay per kilo?'

"'How much do you want?' he asked.

"'I'll let you drink a glass of my plum brandy first,' I said. 'Just one glass and it's on me. Then you'll tell me how much you're willing to give me.'

"'Okay.' In a flash, he downed the brandy I gave him, and his eyes gleamed like knives sharpened for murder.

"'I can tell something about you already,' I said. 'You don't make a good drunk. I can see blood in your eyes and even more blood on your hands. But I may be wrong. Let's not rush to judge; come to my kitchen.' I looked him in the face. 'I'll try another method to test how much you're worth, Mister. You have to drink one more glass of my brandy: I become beautiful after the second glass.'

"'I'm ready to drink four glasses for you,' he said. 'Then you'll be more beautiful than the chicks they have on TV.'

"'That much brandy in your head will do you no good,' I said as he drank the second glass.

"I'll be honest with you, my girl," the woman said, her eyes sinking into mine. "Love only happens after the second glass. Without that second glass, the guy will constantly find faults with you. It'll be your nose that might seem too long, or your legs will be far from perfect, but after the second one the nose will be a treasure and your legs will touch the moon. … Well, the trader's love was nothing much to speak of. Quite a few men have drunk two glasses of my brandy, and one learns to judge a feller by the way he finishes his drink.

"The first glass shows the glow of the fire pit over which he'll roast you once he has you eating out of his hand. Men are wicked, my dear. The second glass tells you if he's got a heart of gold or a puddle of poison in his chest. But the petty trader's heart was neither fish nor fowl. I was at a loss.

"'Look here,' he said. 'I'll pay you as much as you want for half a ton of plums. I'll pay you as much as you want even if I don't buy the plums. The only thing I care about is drinking two more glasses of brandy with you.'

"'No,' I said. 'I don't like you, mister, and I won't make a secret of it. Half a ton costs one thousand levs, but I'll take two thousand from you. And this is to make you go home. Good bye.'

"'How come? I don't want to go. I've fallen in love with you,' he said. 'Your brandy's strong. It gives me so much power that I can't tell if I'm walking on the clouds or along the street to my grandmother's place.'

"'Okay then. Give me the money and you'll have the plums: two grand.'

"'I don't have that much.'

"'Then why are you wasting my time? You've already guzzled my brandy.'

"'It's because I like you so much.'

"'You're a tasteless fool,' I told him.

"I took all his cash. It was as simple as that. I carefully searched his pockets, extracting every bill or coin I could lay my hands on. That's all a man deserves; fleece him, take his money and send him to another woman. Let her wash his socks and listen to the claptrap he'll be babbling day and night."

"I respect my husband," I muttered under my breath. "He's kind-hearted."

"Yes, he's kind-hearted as long as he doesn't meet a mademoiselle blonder than you, my dear. She'll grab his money then they'll drink two glasses of brandy together, and you'll be ironing his shirts. He'll say he's unhappy and you'll be expected to wipe away his tears for him.

"Now listen to the end of my story, and you'll learn a thing or two.

"'I won't go home,' the petty trader repeated.

"I tell you, my dear girl, you must respect the brandy we make in the town of Pernik. After the second glass the guy falls in love with you, and after his third he'd die for you. However, love only happens to living men, doesn't it? So, I collected his trousers, his shirt and jacket, rolled them into a ball, and tossed everything in the street.

"'I'm not a hotel manager and there's no room for you here. Good bye.' That was what I told him.

"On the following day the guy came to my shop.

"'You are very pretty,' he stammered. 'You are! Let's drink two more glasses.'

"'I've already sold the plums to another man,' I informed him.

"'Did he drink brandy with you?'

"'Yes.'

"The petty trader burst into tears. His cheeks shone wet and red and his closed eyelids fluttered; he was a pitiful sight. I'd been selling plums for five years, and many a time I had drunk two glasses of brandy with the most handsome buyers, but none of them had ever sobbed like this.

"'You are a peach!' the buyers would say, but I never took the bait.

"Remember, it's the brandy that's a peach, not you. You can apply a truckload of make-up to your face, spread a layer of *fond de teint* a foot deep on your pores and set your nose in plaster of rouge, and it will be all for naught. It's your plums that count.

"'Do you run your own business?' I probed hard for additional information about him.

"'No,' he said.

"'Do you have money?' I dug deeper into the matter.

"'No. You took everything I had.'

"'Do you have a house?'

"'No,' he said.

"'Do you have anything at all?'

"He spoke up, choking on his own tongue:

"'I look at you and I need no money, no house, no plums, no business. Nothing…'

"'You're crazy,' I said.

"'Yes, I am,' he said.

"'You are not worth a penny,' I accused him.

"'I'm not,' he agreed.

"'What will I do with you?' I wondered.

"'Drink two glasses with me,' he suggested.

"Was it his tears or his foolishness that made his eyes shine like the sun and the moon?

"'You are very pretty,' he said.

"We drank brandy, one glass then another, and from then on, my dear girl, I knew for sure: all men are stones. It's you who decides if you'll lug your man about tied to your neck all your life or throw him in the mud and step on his head to keep your evening shoes clean.

There is still a third option: you'll drink two glasses of brandy with the guy, and like I did, you'll give birth to his children, all three of them, pretty like the sun and the moon. And there's something else, girl. Every time I look at the mirror, I say to myself: *he's judged correctly, yes, I'm pretty*.

"Therefore, my dear, all men are stones, but only one amongst them all is a precious stone. He is your man. The way he dresses shows that he has no taste. He is wild and, frankly, you don't think he has the skills to operate a business, but he is your gemstone. Take care of him.

"Now, run to the nearest supermarket and buy a bottle of brandy. Two glasses are enough, not a drop more, not one!"

A PARTIAL LIST OF SNUGGLY BOOKS

Milton Keynes UK
Ingram Content Group UK Ltd.
UKHW030745040924
447871UK00004B/59